2

Goldilocks Rap

by Clare De Marco

Illustrated by Andy Rowland

W

FRANKLIN WATTS
LONDON•SYDNEY

First published in 2009 by
Franklin Watts
338 Euston Road
London
NW1 3BH

Franklin Watts Australia
Level 17/207 Kent Street
Sydney
NSW 2000

Text © Clare De Marco 2009
Illustration © Andy Rowland 2009

A CIP catalogue record for this book is available
from the British Library.

ISBN 978 0 7496 9186 8 (hbk)
ISBN 978 0 7496 9192 9 (pbk)

Series Editor: Jackie Hamley
Editor: Melanie Palmer
Series Advisor: Dr Barrie Wade
Series Designer: Peter Scoulding

Printed in China

Franklin Watts is a division of
Hachette Children's Books,
an Hachette UK company.
www.hachette.co.uk

A girl called Goldilocks
with long, golden hair

went out for a walk in
the cool morning air.

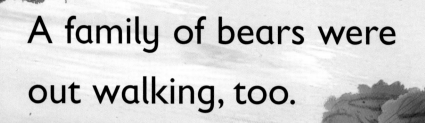

A family of bears were
out walking, too.

5

Goldilocks found
their house.

What did she do?

She smelled something
nice, so she walked inside.

8

She found three bowls
of porridge laid out on
the side.

As she tried the first bowl,
her cheeks went red.

"Ouch! This is too hot!"
Goldilocks said.

11

Then she tried the
second bowl.
"Yuck! Too cold for me!

But what about the little bowl that I can see."

"Yum, yum!" she said
and ate up the whole lot.

"That porridge was just right, not too cold, not too hot."

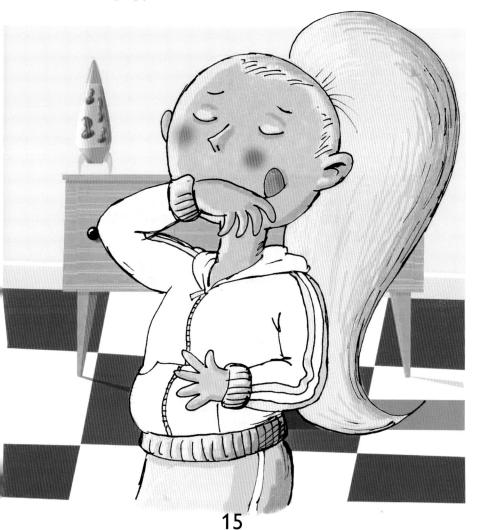

Goldilocks felt sleepy.

Three chairs she saw:

One too hard,

one too soft,

and one smashed
on the floor!

19

She climbed up the stairs
and found a big bed.

"Ouch, much too hard!"
she said, hitting her head.

She tried the second bed.
"Much too soft for me!

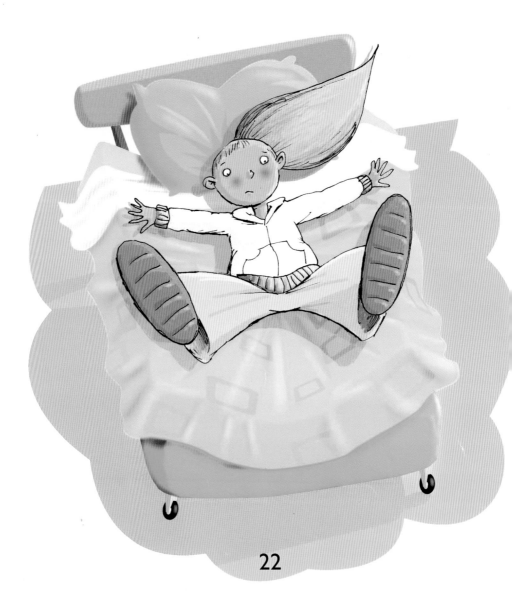

But what about that little
bed that I can see?"

She got into the little bed.
"It's just right!" she cried.

She fell fast asleep. Then
the door opened wide ...

A surprised Baby Bear
asked, "Who are you?"

"I'm Goldilocks,"
she stammered,
"It's nice to meet you."

27

She and Baby Bear were friends for evermore.

Now she doesn't just walk in – she knocks on the door!

Puzzle 1

Put these pictures in the correct order.
Now retell the story in your own words.
Is there a lesson in the story?

Puzzle 2

hair	fair
share	gold

chair	tear
bear	rug

pot	spoon
forgot	hot

Find the non-rhyming word in each word box. Can you think of some words to rhyme with the odd one out?

Answers

Puzzle 1

The correct order is: 1f, 2b, 3e, 4d, 5a, 6c

Puzzle 2

The odd words out are:

gold, rug, spoon.

Look out for more Leapfrog Rhyme Time:

*hardback

For more Leapfrog books go to: www.franklinwatts.co.uk